Drum, Chavi, Drum!
¡Toca, Chavi, Toca!

Story / Cuento
Mayra L. Dole

Illustrations / Ilustraciones
Tonel

Children's Book Press / Editorial Libros para Niños

"Mr. Gonzalez!"
I yell at my music teacher from the other side of the playground,

"Can't I pleeeeease play the congas for the *Calle Ocho* festival tomorrow?"

More than anything, I want to drum on our school's float.

He scrunches up his already wrinkly forehead. "You, my dear," he mumbles as he rakes his hair back, "are a girl." Right! As if I didn't already know that.

"So?" I say. "I can play better than any boy." His thick glasses slide down his nose. "I already chose Carlitos."

I'm mad.
I'll show him I can play better than Carlitos.

—¡Señor González!—
Le grito a mi maestro de música desde el otro lado
del patio escolar.

—**Por favoooooor**, deme permiso
de tocar las tumbadoras en
el festival de la calle Ocho.

Lo que más quiero en el mundo
es tocarlas en la carroza de la escuela.

El maestro arruga la frente. —Corazón de melón,
tú eres hembra —me dice a la vez que se acomoda
el pelo. Como si yo no lo supiera.

—¿Y qué? Pero si yo toco mejor que cualquier
varón —insisto. Los espejuelos de lente
de botella se le resbalan por la nariz.
—Ya escogí a Carlitos.

Estoy brava.
Le voy a demostrar que sé
tocar mejor que Carlitos.

3

I drum fast and hard with two sticks on the sofa arm:

TUN-TUN-chicky-prack! Mami covers her ears.

"¡Niña! That noise is driving me crazy!"
Mami takes the sticks away from me and throws them in the trash.
"I'm the best player ever," I tell her, "but you don't even care."
I grab two soup spoons and a big pot and run out to the porch.
Chicky-CHACK-prack! Abuelito complains, "Chavita,
por favor, drumming is for boys!"

"Please, listen," I beg, "I can really play."
"*Mijita,*" Abuelita pleads. "Our ears will explode."

No one listens; no one believes in me.

Tamborileo bien rápido y bien duro con dos palitos en el brazo del sofá:

¡TUN-TÚN-chiqui-prác! Mami se tapa los oídos.

—**¡Niña!** Esa bulla me está volviendo loca!

Me quita los palitos y los tira en la basura.
—¡Soy la mejor tamborera del mundo entero! —le aseguro.
—Pero tú ni me haces caso.

Agarro dos cucharones y una cazuela grande
y arranco hacia el balcón.

¡Chiqui-CHAC-prác! Abuelito se queja:
—¡Chavita, por favor, los tambores son para los varones!

—Por favor, óiganme —les pido—. ¡De verdad que sé tocar!
—Mijita —me ruega Abuelita— se nos revientan los oídos.

No hay nadie que me oiga, nadie que crea en mí.

Mami is off to work. I kiss the tip of her nose and tap her cheeks with open palms:

Tippy-**TAP**-chicky-**CHACK!**

"Today I'm playing *tumbadoras* at the *Calle Ocho* festival," I tell her. "They're my favorite drums!"

"No way, Chavita!" she reminds me. "The house needs cleaning." Mami works in a *fábrica* making coats, then she gets home and cooks. We eat, and she goes off to another *fábrica*. On weekends she works at the bakery. I'm the only one here who can help her. When Papi was still alive, we were a happy family. Mami didn't work so hard. We listened to music, danced, and laughed a lot. Nothing is the same anymore.

Mami sale para el trabajo. Le doy un besito en la puntica de la nariz y le tamborileo un son en los cachetes con las manos:

¡Tipi-**TAP**-chiqui-**CHÁC!**

—¡Hoy voy a tocar las tumbadoras en el festival de la calle Ocho! —le digo.

—**¡De eso, nada-monada!** Hay que limpiar la casa —regaña Mami. Mami trabaja en una fábrica que hace abrigos, llega a la casa, cocina, comemos y ella se vuelve a ir a otra fábrica. Durante el fin de semana, trabaja en la panadería. Y yo soy la única que puede ayudarla aquí. Cuando Papi estaba vivo, éramos felices. Mami no trabajaba tan duro. Oíamos música, bailábamos, jugábamos y nos reíamos en cantidad. Nada está igual; todo ha cambiado.

My aunt Nini is lying in bed, in her dark, sad room that smells like minty medicine. She's been sick a long time and she never leaves her room. I race into her room and drum on her night table:

Pa-ta-PA, tippy-TAP!

She whispers, "Chavita, *mariposita,* my head hurts." "I'm sorry, Tia Nini." I kiss her forehead. "I'm off to Rosario's," I say, but I don't tell her anything about going to the festival.

I'm on my own all day. I figure I'll get home right before Mami, and speed-clean the house then.

Tía Nini está acostada en su cuarto, un cuarto oscuro
y triste que huele a medicinas mentoladas. Lleva muchísmo
tiempo enferma y ahora nunca sale de su cuarto.
Entro a la carrera y le tamborileo en la mesita
de noche:

¡Pa-ta-PÁ, tipi-TÁP!

Tía Nini murmura: —Chavita, mariposita,
me duele la cabeza.
—Perdóname, Tía Nini. —Le doy un besito
en la frente—. Me voy en casa de Rosario
—le digo, pero no le digo nada de que voy
al festival.

Voy a estar sola toda el día. Pienso que si llego a casa justo
antes de Mami, puedo limpiar la casa en un dos por tres.

9

When I reach Rosario's house, she's cutting a neighbor's hair out on the porch while her dad chases loose chickens around the yard.

Rosario's mom Elsa, our *barrio* manicurist, has her table set up with bottles of fingernail polish; she's doing another neighbor's nails.

"Eh, Chavi!"
Everyone's happy to see me. *"Oye, ¿qué pasa?"* I say hello and spread my little kisses all around.

I sit on the porch steps and tap on an empty paint can:

Tun-DUN-DUN-tun,
chicky-
chack-
PRACK!

"Cool sounds," Rosario says. Her scissors **snippy-snap** to my rhythm.

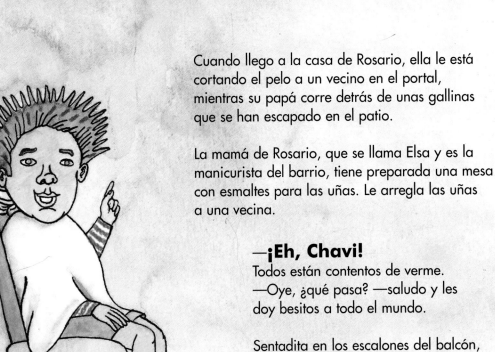

Cuando llego a la casa de Rosario, ella le está cortando el pelo a un vecino en el portal, mientras su papá corre detrás de unas gallinas que se han escapado en el patio.

La mamá de Rosario, que se llama Elsa y es la manicurista del barrio, tiene preparada una mesa con esmaltes para las uñas. Le arregla las uñas a una vecina.

—¡Eh, Chavi!
Todos están contentos de verme.
—Oye, ¿qué pasa? —saludo y les doy besitos a todo el mundo.

Sentadita en los escalones del balcón, empiezo a tamborilear en una lata vacía de pintura:

¡Tun-DUN-DÚN-tun,
chiqui-
chac–
PRÁC!

—¡Suena bien *cool!* —dice Rosario mientras me sigue el compás **—zipi-zap—** con las tijeras.

We zoom off
to *el festival.* Rosario looks great
in her Gloria Estefan mask and outfit.
I'm unrecognizable in a Zorro mask,
a felt *sombrero,* and a long black cape.
We're off to have fun. Mami doesn't
get home till six!

We whiz by Adela, the *Botánica* owner,
who is wearing her white gown, huge
turban, and seven beaded necklaces.
I drum on her store window with my
fists and Rosario **shakes** her shoulders
and hips to the rhythm, sort of like
a washing machine.

Pa-ta-
PA,
chicky-
CHACK!

¡Zuuuum! Salimos a carrera, rumbo al festival. Rosario se ve chévere en su máscara y disfraz de Gloria Estefan. A mí, nadie me va a reconocer detrás de la máscara de Zorro, el sombrero de felpa y la capa larga y negra que llevo. Vamos a divertirnos. ¡Mami no llega hasta las seis de la tarde!

Volamos por donde está Adela, la dueña de la botánica, la señora muy vestida de blanco, con un inmenso turbante y siete collares. Con los puños cerrados tamborileo un ritmo sabroso en la ventana, mientras que Rosario **sacude** los hombros y las caderas al compás del son. Parece una máquina de lavar.

¡Pa-ta-PÁ, chiqui-CHÁC!

13

We laugh our heads off. We **swish-swash** by *El Parque de dominó*, waving at our friends' grandfathers as they sip their *cafecitos* and play dominos. I play on the hood of a parked car with my knuckles:

Goh-doh-**PA**, tun-**PA**, **PA**-ta-**PA**, gun-**DUN!**

"Beautiful rhythm," old Don Pablo says. He taps his feet and snaps his fingers. "It takes me back to Cuba. I'm amazed such a young boy can play such big sounds."

"You're *fantástico!*"

A carcajadas, **cha-cha-chamos** por el Parque de dominó y saludamos a los abuelitos de nuestros amigos, que se toman el cafecito y juegan dominó. Toco con los puños cerrados en el capó de un carro estacionado:

¡Go-do-PÁ, tun-PÁ! ¡PA-ta-PÁ, gun-DÚN!

—¡Qué ritmo tan precioso —me dice el viejito don Pablo. Menea los pies y chasquea los dedos. —Es casi como si estuviera en Cuba. ¿Cómo es posible que este jovencito tenga un ritmo tan maravilloso?

¡Qué fantástico, mijo!

15

"A boy?" Rosario blares. I pull off my mask and hat.
My hair cascades down to my shoulders.

"**Bah**, it's Chavi," the men puff. Don Pablo scolds,
"Girls don't play drums. That's for boys and men!"

Rosario puts her hands on her hips. **"Not so!"**

"Yeah!" I echo. My voice is as loud as a drum.
"Girls can do anything. And I'm so good, I fooled you."

Don Pablo rolls his eyes. "You shouldn't be doing
boy stuff. Your hands will get callused."
All the grandfathers agree.

"I can see that you are going to give your poor mother
a lot of problems," says one of them.

—¿Un jovencito? —chilla Rosario. Me quito la careta y el sombrero.
El pelo me cae en ondas hasta los hombros.

—**Bah**, si es Chavi —dicen los hombres y don Pablo nos regaña—
¡las niñas no tocan tambores. Eso es para los varones
y para los hombres!

Rosario se pone las manos en la cintura. —**¡Eso no es verdad!**

—**¡Claro que no!** —digo yo. La voz me suena como
un tambor—. Nosotras las niñas mujeres podemos hacer cualquier cosa.
Toco tan bien que los engañé a ustedes.

El viejito don Pablo se desespera. —No te conviene hacer cosas de varón.
Te van a salir callos en las manos. —Todos los abuelos están
de acuerdo.

—No cabe duda que le vas a traer muchos dolores de cabeza
a tu pobre madre —dice uno.

"Come with me," Don Pablo insists in his grandfatherly voice. Rosario stands up for me. **"She didn't do anything wrong!"** she insists, as he grabs my arm and starts pulling me to my mother's workplace.

When we get to the factory, Don Marcos, my mom's boss, greets us with a kiss and two *merenguitos.* As he laughs, his gigantic belly ripples.

I see Mami on her knees, scrubbing the floors. My heart stops. I don't like to see her working so hard. **"What happened?"** Mami looks concerned.

Don Pablo tattles. "She was about to roam the festival."

"*Niña!*" Mami is mad.
"What am I going to do with you?"

—Ven conmigo —me dice don Pablo en su voz de viejito.
Rosario me defiende—. **Ella no ha hecho nada malo**
—dice mientras que el viejito me lleva por el brazo hasta
llegar al trabajo de Mami.

El jefe, don Marcos, nos saluda cuando llegamos a la fábrica y
nos da un besito y dos merenguitos a cada una. Cuando se ríe,
la barriga se le menea.

Veo a Mami, que está arrodillada restregando el piso.
Se me para el corazón. No me gusta verla trabajar
tan duro. **—¿Qué pasó?** —pregunta Mami, alarmada.

Don Pablo le cuenta el chisme. —Se la traje antes
de que ella se fuera sola al festival.

—¡Niña! —me regaña Mami—.
¿Qué voy a hacer contigo?

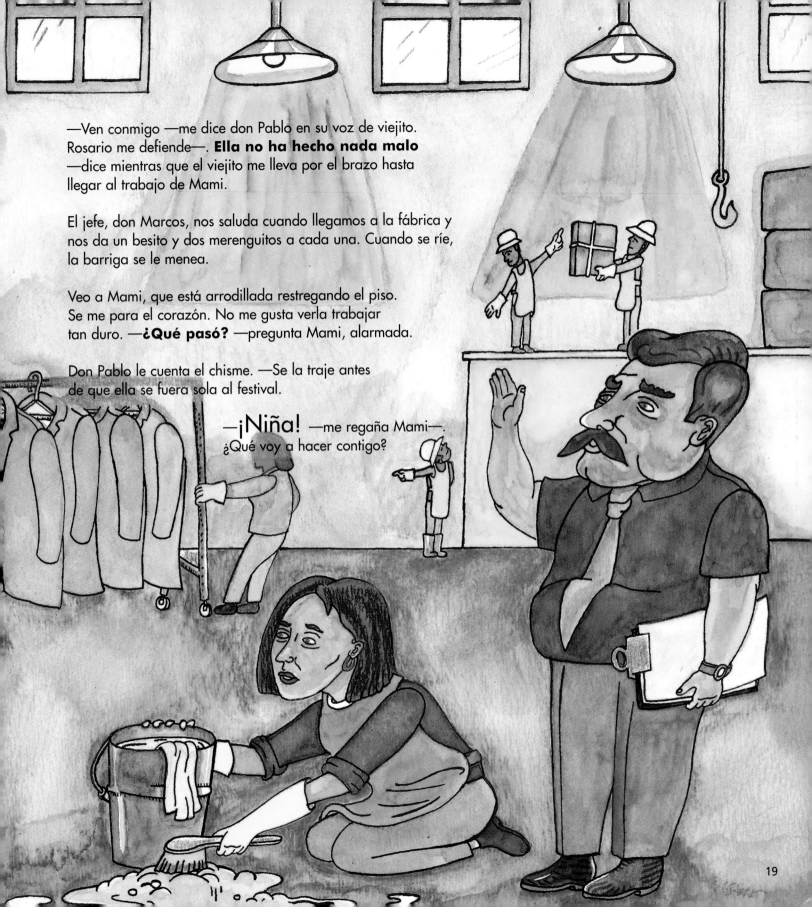

I can't stop thinking about Mami on her knees,
working so hard to make money so we can
eat and pay our bills. Suddenly, tears start
pouring out of me like out of an open faucet.

Mami's really upset now. I've embarrassed her in front of her boss and the neighbors.
"You're punished. No festival for you, young lady!"

Don Marcos's cheeks puff out as if they
were stuffed with donuts. "Esmeralda," he
says to Mami, "all Chavi wants is to have a
good time. Why don't you take the rest of
the day off and go with her?"

Mami reconsiders—she's such
a softy—and turns to Don Marcos.
"Gracias!" she says, beaming.

Todavía estoy pensando en Mami de rodillas, trabajando tan duro para ganar un poquito de dinero y pagar las cuentas. De pronto se me salen las lágrimas como si tuviera abierta una llave de agua.

Ahora sí que Mami está brava. La avergoncé delante del jefe y los vecinos.

—Estás castigada. **¡Se te acabó el festival!**

A don Marcos se le inflan los cachetes como si los tuviera llenos de donas. —Pero Esmeralda —le dice a Mami— lo único que quiere la niña es ir al festival. Vete con ella. Tienes libre el resto de la tarde.

Mami todavía tiene sus dudas pero, ¡es tan fácil de convencer!
—**¡Gracias!** —le dice a don Marcos, radiante de alegría.

We elbow our way through the *Calle Ocho* crowd to our school's float. Mami helps Rosario and me climb on. The festival queen waves and smiles. Carlitos plays congas while a group of my girlfriends dance the *Mozambique,* and sing, *Mírala que linda viene, mírala que linda va...*

Giant animal-shaped balloons shake in the air, and people on stilts drape bright-colored banners, like windblown hair, over the crowd.

Looking down, waving at Mami, we see lots of our *barrio* neighbors selling Cuban flags, fried pork, *pastelitos,* and T-shirts with the map of Cuba.

Rosario sneaks a set of bongos to me.

"Show them what you've got, girl!"

A codazos y cabezazos por la calle Ocho llegamos a la carroza de la escuela. Mami nos ayuda a Rosario y a mí a montarnos. La reina del festival saluda y sonríe. Carlitos toca las tumbadoras y un grupo de mis amigas bailan el *mozambique* y cantan,

Mírala que linda viene, mírala que linda va...

Globos gigantescos en forma de animales giran en el aire, hombres y mujeres en zancos cuelgan banderas de colores, que vuelan sobre la gente como si fueran melenas de pelo largo.

Desde arriba saludamos a Mami y vemos a los vecinos del barrio, que venden banderitas cubanas, masitas de puerco fritas, pastelitos y camisetas con el mapa de Cuba.

Rosario me pasa un bongó.

—¡Demuéstrales lo que sabes, chica!

23

I kneel next to Carlitos. The crowd hushes.
I adjust my Zorro hat and mask, and begin:

Tun-TUN-dun-TUN!

I play with all my heart, with my blood and bones.
My hands are going really fast.

People **cheer**, **clap**, and **stomp** their feet to my beat.
Mr. Gonzalez, the music teacher, storms up to me,
but I can't stop playing. He yells into my ear
and the microphone picks up the sound, "You're
a wonderful drummer, young man, but you must
leave now; you don't belong to our school."

I take off my hat and mask with pride.
"Surprise, surprise!" Rosario trumpets.
The crowd gasps, **"He's a girl!"**

Me arrodillo al lado de Carlitos. La gente se va callando. Me acomodo el sombrero de Zorro y la máscara y empiezo a tocar:

¡Tun-TÚN-dun-TÚN!

Toco con todo el corazón, con la sangre y con los huesos. Muevo las manos con una rapidéz increíble.

El gentío se **anima, aplaude**; todos **mueven los pies** y menean las caderas al compás del tambor. El señor González, el maestro, se me acerca, pero yo no puedo dejar de tocar. Me grita en el oído y el micrófono le recoge la voz: —Tocas muy bien, jovencito, pero tienes que dejar de tocar en esta carroza. Tú no eres de esta escuela.

Me quito el sombrero y la máscara con mucho orgullo.
—**¡Sorpresa! ¡Sorpresa!** —grita Rosario.
Asombrada, la gente exclama: —**¡Es una niña!**

The throng cheers even louder now, **"*Toca,* drummer girl! Play!"** I walk to the congas and bongo drums and start:

Tun-tun, CHICKY-PRACK!

I'm half-dreaming; my eyes are closed. I remember Papi dancing with Mami on Sunday afternoons, and I take out all my sadness and happiness on the drum; it knows what I'm feeling and I become one with it.

The crowds are dancing. Mami throws her hands up in the air and screams, **"That's my daughter!"**

I play like never before:

Dun-dun-TUN-DUN, chicky-PACK- PACK-PRACK!

People throw confetti and unleash striped crepe paper streamers in the air; bright colors fly all over me!

La multitud vuelve a gritar y a aplaudir: —¡Toca, bongosera! ¡Toca!
Me acerco a las tumbadoras y al bongó y empiezo a tocar:

¡Tun-tun, CHIQUI-PRÁC!

Medio-soñando, con los ojos cerrados, me acuerdo de cómo
era cuando Papi y Mami bailaban los domingos por la tarde,
y el tambor repica con esta tristeza y esta alegría. El tambor
sabe lo que siento; somos uno, el tambor y yo.

La gente da vueltas y baila. Mami alza los brazos y grita:
—**¡Esa niña es mía!**

Toco como nunca he tocado:

¡Dun-dun-TUN-DÚN! ¡Chiqui-PAC-PAC-PRÁC!

¡La gente me tira confeti y serpentinas; una nube de colores brillantes vuela sobre mí!

Mami runs to me. She's laughing in colors, like splashes of yellow and red raining over the festival. She takes my face in her hands, "I'm sorry I never listened, *mijita*," and I kiss the tear rolling down her cheek.

Dr. Almeida, the principal, scolds Mr. Gonzalez, "Shame on you! How could you not have allowed Chavi to play?"
She turns to me. "Chavita, you'll be our star *tumbadora* player for as long as you're in our school."

"Super cool!" Rosario and I scream in unison.

Dr. Almeida tells me, **"You're the first girl to play the congas in the history of the *Calle Ocho* festival. And now I want you to keep on playing!"**

Mami se me acerca; se ríe en colores, como si su risa salpicara de rojo y amarillo el festival. Me toma la cara entre las manos. —¡Siento mucho no haberte escuchado antes, mijita! —y yo le beso la lágrima que le rueda por el cachete.

La doctora Almeida, que es directora de la escuela, se pone a regañar al señor González: —¡Qué vergüenza! ¿Cómo es posible que usted no dejara que Chavita tocara el tambor?

Y a mí me dice: —Chavita, en la carroza del año que viene vas a ser la *tumbadorista* principal y de ahí en adelante, igual.

—¡Coolísimo! —chillamos Rosario y yo.

La doctora Almeida me dice:

—Eres la primera tumbadorista niña en la historia del festival de la calle Ocho. Adelante, mija, sigue tocando para nosotros.

The float parades along *Calle Ocho.* People cheer,
clap their hands, and wave as I play my *tumbadoras.*

Rosario sways her hips fast, from side to side. My hands can't stop.

TUN-chicky-prack! Gun-DUN-chicky-prack!

TUN-chicky-prack!

Gun-DUN-chicky-prack!

Mami claps to the beat and shakes her head around and around.
Nothing is better than the feeling I get from seeing Mami happy.
I'm playing for her, for everything she's ever done for me.

Rosario winks at me. She knows, everybody knows that
I was born to play drums!

La carroza pasea a lo largo de la calle Ocho. La gente me saluda de nombre y me aplaude alegremente mientras toco las tumbadoras.

Rosario menea las caderas rapidísimo, de un lado al otro. Mis manos no dejan de tocar.

¡TUN-chiqui-prac! ¡Gun-DÚN-chiqui-prác!

¡TUN-chiqui-prác!

¡Gun-DÚN-chiqui-prác!

Mami aplaude y mueve la cabeza de aquí a allá al compás del tambor. No hay nada que me emocione más que ver a Mami contenta. Toco para ella, por todo lo que siempre ha hecho por mi.

Rosario me guiña un ojo. Ella sabe lo que saben todos, **¡que yo nací para tocar los tambores!**

31

The *Calle Ocho* festival is Miami's biggest street party and the largest Latino festival in the nation. It delights over a million people a year. This *fiesta* brings Cubans together to celebrate our culture and welcome other Latinos and non-Latinos to our world. Visitors enjoy Latin American foods, Latino bands, live performers, dancing, and visual art displays. I chose the festival (and the parade that once was part of it) as the background for my story because it bursts with the *salsita* and *alegría* that characterize Miami's Cuban culture.

—*Mayra L. Dole*

Mayra L. Dole was born in Marianao, Cuba, and raised in a Cuban *barrio* minutes from Miami. Her mother says that, soon after birth, Mayra made drumming gestures with her little hands. Later, as an adult, she played the Senegalese *djembe* drum in a women's band. In addition to being a musician, she has also been a dancer, landscape designer, and hairdresser and is now a prolific writer and spokesperson for the differently-abled. *Drum, Chavi, Drum!* is her first published book.

This book is dedicated to Mami, Damarys, Papi and Nina (¡que en paz descansen!), Popi, Meli, Ita, Polito, Eddie, Martica, Tia Nana, Tia Kika, Beba, Buffaloni, Peggy, Ian, and to all the children and adults with CFIDS/MCS. To children of various colors, races, disabilities, nationalities, and religions: follow your dreams, even if you play to a different beat!
— *Mayra L. Dole*

Tonel is a visual artist and art critic who was born in Havana, Cuba, where he designed posters and published illustrations for magazines and newspapers. His work has been exhibited in North and South America, the Caribbean, and Europe. He received a Rockefeller Foundation Fellowship in the Humanities (1997–1998) and a John S. Guggenheim Foundation Fellowship for painting and installation art (1995). He is now a visiting artist and a professor at the Center for Latin American Studies at Stanford University in California.

For my son Mario Antonio; for my nieces Gretel and Greicy. For all children who enjoy music.
— *Tonel*

Story copyright © 2003 by Mayra L. Dole
Illustrations copyright © 2003 by Tonel

Editors: Ina Cumpiano and Dana Goldberg
Design and production: Tenazas Design, San Francisco
Native Reader: Laura Chastain
Cuban Reader: Antonio E. Fernández
Copy Editor: Rosalyn L. Sheff

Our thanks to the staff of Children's Book Press.
Printed in Singapore by Tien Wah Press.
10 9 8 7 6 5 4 3 2 1
Distributed to the book trade by Publishers Group West.
Quantity discounts are available through the publisher
for educational and nonprofit use.

Children's Book Press is a nonprofit publisher of multicultural
literature for children, supported in part by grants from the
California Arts Council. Write us for a complimentary catalog:
Children's Book Press, 2211 Mission Street, San Francisco, CA 94110;
415.821.3080. Visit our website at www.childrensbookpress.org

California
Arts Council

Library of Congress Cataloging-in-Publication Data

Dole, Mayra L.
        Drum, Chavi, Drum! / story, Mayra L. Dole;
illustrations, Tonel = ¡Toca, Chavi, toca! / cuento,
Mayra L. Dole; ilustraciones, Tonel.
        p. cm.
        Summary: Chavi's music teacher believes that
only boys should play drums in Miami's Festival de la Calle
Ocho, but Chavi knows she is a good musician and looks
for a way to prove it.
        ISBN 0-89239-186-3
        [1. Sex role—Fiction. 2. Drums—Fiction.
3. Festivals—Fiction. 4. Cuban Americans—Fiction. 5. Miami
(Fla.)—Fiction. 6. Spanish language materials—Bilingual.] I.
Title: ¡Toca, Chavi, toca!. II. Tonel, ill. III. Title.

PZ73 .D6555 2003
[E]—dc21
2002036696